My Dad's
a Birdman

Other books by David Almond

Skellig
Kit's Wilderness
Heaven Eyes
Counting Stars
Secret Heart
Wild Girl, Wild Boy – A Play
Skellig – A Play
The Fire-Eaters
Clay

DAVID ALMOND

MY DAD'S A BIRDMAN

Illustrated by
POLLY DUNBAR

WALKER
BOOKS

First published 2007 by Walker Books Ltd
87 Vauxhall Walk, London SE11 5HJ

2 4 6 8 10 9 7 5 3 1

Text © 2007 David Almond
Illustrations © 2007 Polly Dunbar

This book has been typeset in Caslon

Printed in China

British Library Cataloguing in Publication Data:
a catalogue record for this book is available
from the British Library

ISBN 978-1-4063-0486-2

www.walkerbooks.co.uk

For Freya, and for David Lan
D. A.

For my dad
P. D.

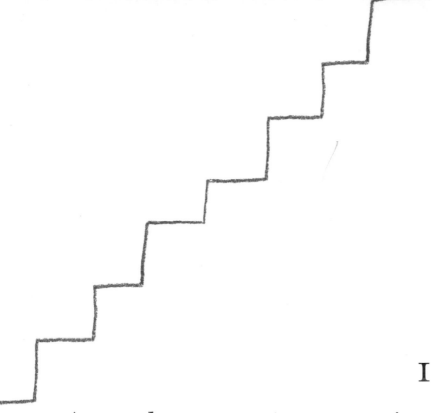

I

An ordinary spring morning

in 12 Lark Lane. The birds were tweeting and whistling outside. The city traffic rumbled and roared. Lizzie's alarm went ringadingding. She jumped out of bed, washed her face, scrubbed behind her ears, brushed her teeth, brushed her hair, put on her uniform, went downstairs, filled the kettle, switched it on, put bread in the toaster, set the table with two plates, two mugs, two knives, milk and butter and jam, then she went to the foot of the stairs.

"Dad!" she shouted. "Daddy!"

No answer.

"Dad! Time to get up!"

No answer.

"If you don't get up now, I'll come up there and…"

She stepped heavily onto the first step, then onto the second step.

"I'm on me way!" she shouted.

She heard a grunt and a groan, then nothing.

"I'll count to five. One … two … two and a half… Daddy!"

There was a muffled shout from upstairs.

"Oriyt, Lizzie! Oriyt!"

There was a crash and another groan, then there he was, in a scruffy dressing-gown and holey slippers and his hair all wild and his face all hairy.

"Downstairs now," said Lizzie.

He stumbled down.

"And don't look at me like that."

"No, Lizzie."

She tugged the dressing-gown straight on his shoulders.

"Look at the state of you," she said. "What on earth have you been doing up there?"

He grinned.

"Been dreaming," he said.

"Dreaming! What a man. Now sit at the table. Sit up straight."

"Yes, Lizzie."

He sat down on the edge of a chair. His eyes were shining and excited. Lizzie poured him a mug of tea. "Drink this," she said, and he took a little sip. "And eat that toast." He nibbled at a corner of the toast. "Eat it properly, Dad." He took a bigger bite. "And chew it," she said. He chewed for a moment. "And *swallow* it, Dad." He grinned. "Yes, Lizzie." He took a big bite, chewed, swallowed, and he opened his mouth wide for her to look inside.

"All gone," he said. "See?"

She clicked her tongue and turned her eyes away. "Don't be silly, Dad," she said. Then she smoothed his hair down and brushed it. She straightened the collar of his pyjama jacket. She felt the thick stubble on his chin.

"You've got to look after yourself," she said. "You can't go on the way you are. Can you?"

He shook his head.

"No, Lizzie," he answered. "Certainly not, Lizzie."

"I want you to have a shower and a shave today and to get properly dressed."

"Yes, Lizzie."

"Good. And what plans have you got for today?"

He sat up straight and looked her in the eye.

"I'm going to fly, Lizzie. Just like a bird."

Lizzie rolled her eyes.

"Are you now?" she said.

"Yes, I am. And I'm going to enter the competition."

"Competition? What competition?"

He laughed and leaned forward and held her arm.

"The Great Human Bird Competition, of course! Have you not heard about it? It's coming to town! I heard about it yesterday. No, the day before yesterday. Or that day a week gone last Tuesday. Anyway, the first one to fly across the River Tyne wins a thousand pounds. And I'm going to enter. It's true, Lizzie. It's really true. I'm going to win! I'm going to make me mark at last."

He stood up and held his arms out straight and flapped them.

"Are me feet off the floor?" he asked. "Are they? Are me feet off the floor?"

He ran and flapped, like he was flying.

"Oh, Dad," said Lizzie. "Don't be silly."

She ran after him. He led her round and round the room. She caught up with him at last, and smoothed his hair down again and straightened his dressing-gown.

"OK," she said. "Mebbe you are going to fly like a bird, but make sure you get some fresh air and get a good lunch inside you, OK?"

He nodded. "OK, Lizzie," he said, and then he flapped again and giggled.

"Oh, and Auntie Doreen said she might pop round today."

That stopped Dad in his tracks. His face crashed

"Auntie Doreen?" he said.

He twisted his face and sighed.

"Not her again!"

"Yes, her again. She'll bring you down to earth."

He stamped his left foot. He stamped his right foot.

"But Lizzie…" he groaned.

"Never mind But Lizzie," said Lizzie. "Auntie Doreen loves you, just like I do. And she worries about you, just like I do. So be nice to her."

His shoulders drooped and his arms dangled by his side. Lizzie got her school bag, then kissed his cheek. She smiled gently and shook her head. He was just like a little boy standing there.

"What am I going to do with you?" she said.

"Don't know, Lizzie," he muttered.

She hesitated.

"I don't know if I should leave you on your own."

He laughed at her.

"Course you should," he said. "You got to go to school and do your sums and your spellings."

He was right. She did need to go to school. She liked school. She liked her sums and her spellings and her teachers, and she liked her head teacher, Mr Mint, who had been so kind to her and to her dad.

"All right," she said. "I'll go. Now give me a kiss bye-bye."

He kissed her cheek. They hugged each other. She held her finger up.

"Now remember," she said.

"Yes, Lizzie. I'll remember. Wash. Shave. Get a good lunch. Get lots of fresh air. And be nice to Auntie D."

"Good. That's right."

"And I'll remember to fly."

"Oh, Dad."

He put his hand to her back and guided her towards the door.

"Go on," he told her. "You haven't a thing to worry about. Off you go to your lovely school."

She opened the door and stepped out into the garden. She peered at him.

"Bye-bye," he said.

"Bye-bye, Dad."

She walked away down the garden and through the garden gate and into the street outside. She stood there for a moment, and looked back at him. "Go *on*," said Dad. "I'm *fine*." She set off walking again. He waved until she was out of sight, then he closed the door. He flapped his arms and started giggling.

"Tweet tweet," he said. He poked a piece of toast out from under his tongue. He spat it out. "Tweet tweet," he said. "Tweet tweet, tweet tweet." Then he saw a fly crawling on the table.

"Yum yum," he said, and he set off after it.

2

The little fly was much too quick for him. It

flew up off the table and buzzed around above his head.
It hung upside down on the ceiling as he tweeted and
puffed and panted and flapped his arms at it.

"I'll get you, you little devil!" he called. "Come on
down and I'll gobble you up."

But it didn't come down, and he didn't gobble it up. He
sat down on the floor getting his breath back. Then he had
another thought, and he started crawling about beside the
skirting board. He scratched the floorboards with his
fingernails and found little black beetles and little brown
bugs and funny white creepy things and he scratched them
out, picked them up and popped them into his mouth.

15

"Yum yum!" he said. "What good's toast to a man like me? A man like me needs bugs and flies and centipedes."

He sat there, and smacked his lips and sighed with joy. He stood up and flapped his arms. He stood at the window and stared out at the garden. He didn't see Lizzie peeping out from behind a tree.

"And a man like me needs worms!" he said. "Look out, little slimy worms! Yum yum! I'll soon be coming out to get you!"

Then he shut up, and his eyes went all glassy, and he smiled so deeply. "If only she knew," he whispered to himself. "If only lovely Lizzie knew." And he reached into his dressing-gown pocket and he took out a key and tip-toed upstairs.

3

He tiptoed into his bedroom,

tiptoed around his bed, and tiptoed to a cupboard that stood against the wall. He put the key into the lock and turned it and ever so gently, ever so carefully, he pulled open the door. He sighed and smiled with joy.

"Come on out, my beauties," he said.

He reached inside, and pulled out a pair of home-made wings.

"They're *gorgeous*," he said. He took off his dressing-gown and put them on over his pyjamas. They were made of feathers and string and bits of old shirt and bits of bamboo and wire and thread and cardboard and feathers and feathers and feathers. "They're just *gorgeous*! Just wait till my Lizzie sees."

He stood on tiptoes. He stretched his arms. He closed his eyes. He dreamed of flying like a swallow, like a swift, like a hawk, high above the house. And as he dreamed, someone started calling from outside.

"Entries for the Human Bird Competition! All entries for the Great Human Bird Competition!"

Dad didn't hear at first, even though the voice was so loud, and even though it echoed through the street and off the walls and off the roofs.

"Just wait till Lizzie sees," he said again. "She'll be so proud."

The voice boomed out again.

"ALL ENTRIES FOR THE HUMAN BIRD COMPETITION!"

"Eh?" grunted Dad. "What's that? She'll say, That's my dad. Isn't he just a marvellous dad?"

The voice boomed out *again*.

"ALL ENTRIES FOR THE GREAT HUMAN BIRD COMPETITION!"

He ran to the window. There was a little chubby man outside the garden gate. He was carrying a clipboard. He held a megaphone to his mouth.

"ALL ENTRIES FOR THE—"

Dad shoved the window open. "Aye!" he yelled. He waved his arms at the little chubby man. "Me, mister! ME!"

And the man stopped calling, and he looked up at the window.

"YOU?" he boomed.

"Aye! Me! Just wait, mister!"

Dad rushed downstairs. He flung the front door open and yelled again.

"ME! ME! ME!"

The little chubby man lowered the megaphone.

He stepped through the gate and came through the garden with his clipboard under his arm. He stepped through the open door and he came into the kitchen. He put his megaphone on the kitchen table. He raised his clipboard. He licked his pencil and looked at Dad. Dad trembled. His wings shivered with excitement. He could hardly breathe.

"So," said the little chubby man. "You wish to enter the Great Human Bird Competition."

"Aye," said Dad. "I mean, yes please, mister."

"My name," said the man, "is Mr Poop."

"Yes please, Mr Poop, sir," said Dad.

Mr Poop gazed at Dad, at his wings, at the room. He licked his pencil again. He held it over a form attached to the clipboard.

"Name?" he asked.

"Jackie," answered Dad.

"Jackie what?"

Dad blinked. He wondered about it. He tried to remember. Then he answered, "My name is Jackie … Crow."

"Are you sure?" said Mr Poop.

"Aye!" said Dad. "I mean yes sir, Mr Poop."

Mr Poop wrote on his clipboard, and as he wrote he

murmured, "Jack-ie C-row. Occupation?"

Dad blinked again, and wondered again, and tried to remember.

"Mr Crow," insisted Mr Poop. "What is your occupation? What job do you do?"

"I'm a birdman!" snapped Dad. "Yes. I'm a birdman. I think I used to do something else, but now I can't quite remember what it was. I'm a birdman!"

Mr Poop licked his pencil. "Bird-man," he muttered as he wrote. "And what is your method of propulsion?"

Dad goggled at him. Method of propulsion? What did the man mean, method of propulsion?

"Eh?" he grunted.

"What is your *method of propulsion*, Mr Crow," said Mr Poop. "How are you going to fly?"

And Dad understood, and shook his shoulders and flapped his wings towards the ceiling.

"Why, with me wings, of course," he said. "Aren't they lovely, Mr Poop?"

He flapped his wings faster. He ran around the room.

"Don't you think they're *wonderful?*"

When Dad stopped and stood red-

faced, puffing and panting, Mr Poop inspected the wings. He touched the feathers gently. He sniffed. He tugged. He pondered. He sighed.

"Well?" said Dad. "Don't you think they're brilliant?"

"Hmmmmmmmmm," said Mr Poop.

"Oh, I know," sighed Dad. "They're not perfect yet. They need a stitch here, a pin there, a nail there, a bit of cardboard there, a few more feathers there. But other-wise…"

"Hmmmmmmmmmmmmmmmmmmmmmm," said Mr Poop again.

"And I'll have a beak and a crest, of course," said Dad.

Mr Poop walked around Dad. He touched. He sniffed. He tugged. He sighed.

"Wings, beak, crest," he murmured.

Dad watched Mr Poop. He listened. He knew that Mr Poop was far from convinced.

"And I've got faith!" said Dad.

Mr Poop looked up.

"Faith, Mr Crow?"

"Aye, faith, Mr Poop. I *know* I can do it, you see. I *believe* I can do it."

Mr Poop pondered again. He tapped his cheek. He licked his pencil. He patted his chubby tummy. And then he spoke.

"The competition will be intense, Mr Crow. They're coming from all around the world. There's a fella from France that's screwed wings to his bike. There's a lass from Japan with a ten-foot pogo stick. There's a bloke from Brazil with an umbrella on his head and a propeller on his bum. They're bringing parachutes and catapults and whizzers and spinners and giant springs and—"

"And I've got me wings and me faith," said Dad.

"Hmmmmm," replied Mr Poop. "You're aware of the dangers? Bumps on the head, broken bones, cuts and bruises, drowning in the river… Falling from the sky is not recommended, Mr Crow."

"Falling!" scoffed Dad. "Give us that pencil."

Mr Poop gave Dad the pencil. He held out the clipboard.

"Sign here, Mr Crow."

Dad signed with a flourish.

"And here," said Mr Poop. "And also here."

Dad signed again, and then again.

Mr Poop inspected the entry form. He signed it himself with a little chubby signature.

"Entry accepted," he said, and Dad gasped with joy and reached out to hug Mr Poop, who moved smartly away.

"We will see you next Sunday," he said. "Take-off is at 10a.m. And I would advise the wearing of a strong helmet. Goodbye."

He lifted his megaphone from the table, slotted the clipboard under his arm. He went back out through the door. Dad watched him go down the garden, go through the gate, disappear into the street outside.

Then Dad watched the birds above.

"Helmet!" he said. "Who needs a helmet? Look at that crow out there. Look at the way it hangs in the air.

Look at the way it flaps and flies so lovely and easy. That's the way to do it!"

And he stood there dreaming, and in his dreams he flew high over the garden, high over the city, high over the River Tyne, and he didn't notice Lizzie slipping out from behind a tree, coming right up to him. He didn't notice her as she stood in front of him and waved her hand in front of his face.

"Dad," she said. "Daddy."

He was lost in his lovely dream of flying. He turned back into the house, closing the door behind him, and he didn't notice Lizzie slip back in at his side.

5

Dad ran around

the room. He flapped his arms. He tweeted and cooed and squeaked and squawked. Lizzie reached out to him as he dashed past. She called to him. But he didn't see her, didn't hear her. She watched him from the corner of the room.

"I'm in the air!" he yelled. "Me feet are off the ground! They are!"

He giggled at himself.

"No they're not, you nitty nutter," he said. "But they will be! A bit more practice. A few more hours! A few more days! *Wheeee!*"

He stuttered to a halt. He bent forward and panted and puffed. He inspected his wings. He fiddled with the feathers and the strings and the clips and the pins. Yes, they were far from perfect. Yes, they needed some adjustments: a little twist here, a little tweak there. But to his eyes they were magic. They were better than propellers or parachutes, better than catapults or pogo sticks. Wings were the things that'd carry him up like a bird into the air, the things that'd bring victory to him, to Jackie Crow of 12 Lark Lane. He hugged himself as he daydreamed of competition day. He saw the others splashing in the river yelling for help while he flapped high above. And he saw Lizzie down there, on the river-bank, looking up at him and waving and yelling out to anyone who'd listen, "That's my dad up there! That's Jackie Crow! My dad's a birdman! He's the greatest bird-man and the greatest dad there's ever been!"

He laughed, and picked up a beetle from the floor. Lizzie gagged as he flicked it into his mouth.

"Yum yum," he said.

He shoved the breakfast things off the table, then quickly climbed up onto it.

"Dad, no!" shouted Lizzie.

"One!" he said. "Two…!"

"Dad! *No!*" yelled Lizzie, and she leapt to save him, but too late.

"Three!" he yelled. "Blast off!"

And he jumped towards the ceiling and crashed down to the floor.

"Ow!" he cried. "Ouch, me back! Aagh, me knee! Ow, me head!"

"Dad, man!" said Lizzie. "You'll kill yourself!"

He giggled through his pain.

"I nearly did it, Lizzie! I was nearly away that time! Did you see us? Me feet were..." He stopped. He goggled at her. "What you doing here, lass?"

She put her arm under his wings and helped him to sit up.

"I'm here because I was worried about you," she said. "And I was right. You could break your back, man."

"Break me back? Don't be daft." He waggled his shoulders. "D'you like me wings, Lizzie? I've been keeping them a secret. They were going to be a big surprise for you."

She touched them, sniffed them.

"Aye," she said. "I suppose they're lovely, Dad, but..."

"There's no supposing about it. These wings is going to make us famous and rich!"

"But, Dad..."

"Anyway, you're supposed to be at school. What about your sums and your spellings? What's Mr Mint going to say?"

Lizzie didn't know what Mr Mint would say, but she knew he'd be concerned. She knew he'd want to find out what was going on.

"Mr Mint's a nice man," she said. "He understands that sometimes I need to stay at home."

She went on inspecting the wings. She looked at the way the string and the feathers and the wires were so carefully woven together. She touched a single feather with her fingertip. It was so smooth, so beautifully formed. She touched another, deep and shining black.

"Is this a blackbird's?" she said.

"Aye, Lizzie, it is."

He took off the wings. They rustled as he lifted them, like trees, like living things. He pointed to other feathers. He showed her a pigeon's feather, and one from a thrush, and one from a magpie. He showed her how big a crow feather is, and how strong seagull feathers are. And he showed her the tiny delicate feather of a linnet, and the sweetly coloured feather of a chiffchaff, and the beautiful feather from sweet little Jenny wren.

And Lizzie smiled as he showed her. And she sighed with him at the beauty of the feathers and the wings. Her dad had always been clever with his hands. He'd always been able to make things; like the doll's house he'd made for her fifth birthday, the puppets and the puppet theatre he'd made that Christmas when she was six. And the

33

swing in the garden, and the
little playhouse that was like a cottage from a
fairy tale. And home-made books, and dolls. But these
wings were something new, something strange, something wonderful.

"They're lovely, Dad," she whispered.

"They're from the garden," said Dad. "It's amazing
what you find lying under the trees. Dropped feathers
everywhere."

"You're so clever," said Lizzie, but she shook her head. "But you're silly as well, Dad. A man can't fly just by putting feathers on."

"Yes he can!" Dad replied. "It's a matter of getting the jumping and the flapping right. Believe in it, and off you go." Then he sighed. "There's just one problem, though."

"What's that?" said Lizzie.

In answer, he got hold of his tummy. He wobbled it. She smiled. He'd always been a bit plump, ever since she could remember.

"*This* is the problem," he said. "Look at this belly, Lizzie. I'm too blooming fat. That's what's holding me back. Did you ever see a fat bird? Did you ever see a wobbly bird?"

Lizzie thought about it. There were those big fat Christmas turkeys that could hardly walk, never mind fly. But they weren't supposed to fly. They were supposed to waddle around eating rich food for a few months then end up stuffed on a Christmas table. And there were those poor dumpy chickens in those tiny cages. And…

Dad saw what she was thinking.

"Did you ever see a wobbly bird that could *fly*?"

She shook her head.

"Course you didn't!" said Dad. "And why is that? It's because of what they eat!"

He picked a tiny beetle from the floor and flicked it into his mouth. Lizzie yelped.

"They eat bugs, flies, berries and seeds and worms," said Dad. "They do not eat rich food. They do not eat toast. And they definitely positively do not eat your Auntie Doreen's dinners!"

He ate another bug.

He went, "Tweet tweet! Tweet tweet!"

A bird whistled from outside.

"See?" he said. "It's working."

He went, "Caw caw! Caw caw!" just like a crow, and a crow cawed back from outside.

"See?" he said. "I'll be a real proper birdman. It's all for you, lass. You'll be so proud of us."

"But Dad," she said softly, and she held him gently by the arm, "I don't need you to be a birdman. I just need you to be my dad."

Dad paused. He looked into Lizzie's eyes.

"Really?" he said, as if the thought had never crossed his mind.

And Lizzie started to speak again, but a voice from outside interrupted her.

"Jack? Jackie!"

Dad flinched.

"Oh no!" he said. "She's here already!"

He jumped up. He cawed like a crow. He ran out into the garden. There was no stopping him.

"Hello little wormies!" he cried.

6

Auntie Doreen burst into the room. She wore a green pinny with red flowers on it. She pulled off her yellow hat. She stamped on the floor with her shiny blue boots. She put a big tartan shopping bag on the table.

"Elizabeth!" she said. "Have you seen that big daft man out there?"

"What big daft man?" asked Lizzie.

"There's just one big daft man round here and it's not me and it's not you. It'll be about that daft competition, is it?"

"Yes, Auntie Doreen."

Auntie Doreen rolled her eyes.

"Human bird indeed," she said. "The whole town's going crackers. People should stick to being people, that's my opinion. Don't you agree, Elizabeth?"

"Yes, Auntie Doreen."

"They should keep their feet on God's good earth. Don't you agree, Elizabeth?"

"Yes, Auntie Doreen."

"Of course you do." Auntie Doreen waddled around the room flapping her arms and squawking like a bird and reaching for the sky to show how stupid it all was.

"See?" she said. "Absolutely no chance whatsoever at all. Birds is birds and human beans is human beans. And I hope they've been teaching you that at—" She stopped. She stared at Lizzie. "Why aren't you at school, me lass?"

Lizzie lowered her eyes. What on earth could she say?

"I'm not well," she said at last.

"You look well enough to me!" said Auntie Doreen. "What's wrong with you?"

"I've got a bad leg," said Lizzie. "No, a bad head. I mean a bad belly." She leaned forward and clutched her tummy. "Oooooh," she groaned. "Bad belly. *Ooooh!*"

Auntie Doreen pursed her lips and narrowed her eyes and believed none of it.

"Bad belly indeed!" she said. "Good home cooking is what you need. And it's what that big daft man needs, an' all. Things is going to rack and ruin here. What's two plus two?"

"Eh?" said Lizzie.

"Don't you mean pardon?"

"Pardon," said Lizzie.

"What's two plus two? I need to see how far you're slipping behind."

"Four."

Auntie Doreen counted up on her fingers.

"Correct!" she said. "At least something's going right. Ever since your poor mam… Ever since, he's been going potty as a pancake." She stumbled over the wings that were lying on the floor. "What's these things?"

Lizzie lifted them up and held them for Auntie Doreen to see.

"They're his wings," she said.

Auntie Doreen goggled at her.

"His wings?" she said. "Oh, pump! It's worse than I thought!" She looked out into the garden and saw Dad out there dangling a worm in front of his face. She gasped with fright. "What on earth's he doing with that poor worm?"

Lizzie looked out as well, and they saw the worm disappear into Dad's mouth.

"It looks like he's eating it, Auntie Doreen."

Auntie Doreen retched, like she was going to be sick.

"Jackie!" she yelled. "Jackie, man! Leave it alone, you nit!" But Dad picked up another worm, and held it up before his face. "Oh no! Oh, blitheration! *Uuuuurgh!*" She closed her eyes and clutched her belly. "What kind of house is this?"

"It's a nice house, of course," said Lizzie.

"It was, once upon a time," said Auntie Doreen. She grabbed Lizzie and hugged her to her massive chest. "Oh you poor poor child."

"I am not a poor child," said Lizzie in a muffled voice.

"Aye you are, and you know you are." Then she pushed Lizzie away and stood up straight. "Put them daft wings away," she commanded.

Lizzie hung them on the back of the door.

"Good. Now it's time to get to work!" said Auntie Doreen. "There's some suet in that shopping bag. Get it out for us, lass. What that man needs is a dumpling!"

7

Auntie Doreen scrubbed the table. Lizzie got suet and eggs and flour out of the shopping bag. She filled a jug of water. She got wooden spoons and a great big mixing bowl. She put them on the table in front of Auntie Doreen. Auntie Doreen threw lots of stuff into the bowl and started stirring and mixing. She kept her eyes away from the window.

"Flying indeed!" she said. "You cannot whack a bit of proper food to bring some sense into a silly world. Suet dumplings, them's the things. Look at them lovely crumbs of fat. Feel them greasy little pieces. Wait till that lovely cooking smell gets going. It'll bring the daftest man winging straight back to his senses. Thump and knead, Doreen! Thump and knead and shape it into lovely balls."

She made a shiny white dumpling, and held it in her fist. She threw it up and caught it. She threw it up again and let it drop to the floor with a thud. She grinned.

"Grand," she said. "That one's solid enough."

She made another one.

"Catch!" she shouted and she lobbed it at Lizzie.

"How's that?" said Auntie Doreen. "It's like a lump of lead. Perfect!" She caught sight of Dad outside, climbing a cherry tree. "Get out of that tree, Jackie, man!" she yelled. "He'll drive us potty as hisself." She made another dumpling. She went to the door and yelled, "Jackie, snap out of it, man!" Dad took no notice. He just went on climbing and tweeting and cawing. Auntie Doreen drew her arm back and hurled the dumpling at Dad. He didn't notice a thing as it flew past him and thudded like a cannonball down onto the lawn. She groaned and closed the door again. "I pray you won't go the same way, our Elizabeth," she said.

"No, Auntie Doreen," said Lizzie.

Auntie Doreen kissed her sloppily on the check.

"Good. Your mam would've been proud of you. I was just saying to your head teacher, Mr Mint—"

"Mr Mint?" said Lizzie.

"Yes, Mr Mint. I was having a word with him. About you and about your silly… He said you're a sweet and sensible girl. Always works hard, he said. Always polite. Good girl. Spell cat."

"Eh?" said Lizzie.

"*Pardon,*" said Auntie Doreen.

"Pardon," said Lizzie.

"Spell cat."

"C-A-T," said Lizzie.

Auntie Doreen smiled.

"That's correct. You'll turn out right as rain. Now, then. More dumplings!"

And she set to work again, and as she worked she started to sing:

"Dumplings! Dumplings! Lovely lovely dumplings!
Mix them, whack them, roll them out and smack them!
Bash them, boil them, bring them out and bounce them!
Dumplings, oh lovely dumplings!"

As she sang, Lizzie danced to the tune. She raised her arms and flapped them and dreamed the silly dream of flying. Auntie Doreen set a big pan of water boiling, and she dropped dumpling after dumpling into it. When they were cooked, she put them on a rack to cool and steam, and the tender smell of dumplings wafted around the kitchen. Suddenly, the door burst open and Dad came running in. He had a carrier bag in his hand and in the bag there was something flipping and flapping and squawking and snapping.

"I caught it!" he yelled. "I caught it, Lizzie! *Yahoo!*"

8

He belted round the room like the bag was dragging him after it. It kept lurching into the air and jittering down to the ground again. He held it tight. His hair flew around his head. His eyes were weird and wild and excited. Once he stopped and tried to look inside the bag but he snapped it shut again and he yelled, "Ouch! Gerroff! I'm just trying to get a look at you!" And the bag set off again, dragging him after it. He stopped again. He held the flapping thing to his face. "Calm down," he said. "Would you like a worm?" But it just squawked and squealed and crackled and flapped, and Dad set off running again. Auntie Doreen stood in front of the dumplings. Lizzie stood stock-still in amazement.

"What on earth are you doing?" said Auntie Doreen at last.

"I caught the crow!" yelled Dad.

"You caught the crow? Pumpety-pump! What you doing catching a crow?"

"It's for research," said Dad. "I want to inspect it and see where I'm going wrong. Ouch! Oooh! Calm down, you daft bird!"

"Let it go, Jackie, man!" said Auntie Doreen.

"It's cruel, Dad," said Lizzie.

"Ouch!" said Dad. "Ooh! I don't mean any harm,

Lizzie." He held it up to his face again. "I want to be your friend," he whispered, but the crow didn't want to be his. It pecked through the bag and its big grey beak jutted out and pecked at Dad's pink nose. Its whole head appeared and it glared out with angry marbly beady eyes. "Hello, crow," said Dad. "I just want to…" But it stabbed his cheek with its beak. It squawked and cawed and flapped. Auntie Doreen screamed in fright.

"Get rid of it, man!" she yelled. "Get it out before it attacks us all!"

Dad ran to the door and flung the bag and the bird into the sky. The bag dropped back and fell onto Dad's head and rested there.

"Bye-bye, crow," he called.

"Jackie," said Auntie Doreen.

"Aye?" said Dad.

"Have a dumpling."

"Eh?" he said.

She lobbed a dumpling at him.

"Have a blooming dumpling," she said.

He caught it, looked at it, smelt it, then threw it out the door.

"It was a lovely bird," he said.

"What you did was cruel," said Lizzie.

"It was looking at me like it wanted to be me pal," Dad continued. "It smiled at me."

"Dad," said Lizzie. "It was cruel."

"D'you think so, Lizzie?" He pondered. "I suppose it didn't really seem too chuffed."

"Dumpling," said Auntie Doreen. She lobbed another one at him. He stepped out of the way and it went sailing out of the door and bounced across the garden. She glared at him. "Right," she said. "Enough's enough. That's it." She put her hat back on. She dusted the flour off her hands. "Elizabeth, get your coat. You're coming with me."

But Lizzie ignored Auntie Doreen and went to her dad's side.

"You could just watch the birds, Dad," she said. "You could look at them in the garden. You could make notes and drawings. You don't really need to catch them, do you?"

He looked at the ground.

"Suppose not," he muttered.

She pointed into the sky, at a crow that was flapping high over the garden.

"Look at that crow," she said. "Can you see there's feathers sticking out like fingers at the back of its wings? You haven't got them on your wings, have you?"

"No, I haven't," said Dad.

"Lizzie!" snapped Auntie Doreen. "Come here!"

But Lizzie wasn't listening. She pointed into the sky again. "And look at that lovely little wren," she said. "Oh, and listen to the songs, Dad."

They looked and listened together. There were birds in the sky and in the trees.

There were birds on
rooftops and walls
and on chimney pots,
and their singing was
everywhere and it was so beautiful.

"Aren't they lovely?" said Lizzie.

"Just lovely," said Dad.

They listened together, then he whistled and a bird
whistled back. He cawed and a bird cawed back.

"You're so clever, Dad," murmured Lizzie.

"Elizabeth!" snapped Auntie Doreen. "Get your coat
on now!"

"Oh, and look," said Lizzie. "Can you see those two
little sparrows?"

Dad smiled. Auntie Doreen just watched, didn't
know what to say.

"Aye," he said. "Look, there's another one! Three little
sparrows." They watched the sparrows hopping across the
garden. "There's a whole little family of them."

"And look at them swallows," said Lizzie. "Look how
they've got little pointy feathers
on their tails. You haven't
got them, have you?"

Dad shook his head.

51

"Mebbe you just need some extra work on the wings, Dad. A twist here, an extra feather there, and you'll be up and away." She gave him a cuddle. "Hey, Dad," she said, "mebbe I can help you."

Dad's eyes widened. He grinned. He was overjoyed.

"Would you really help us?" he said.

She smiled. Of course she would help. It'd be like when she'd helped him paint the playhouse, or when she'd helped put the final touches to the puppets. It'd be like when they'd planted that little ash tree in the garden together, when Dad had said they made a great team.

"Course I would," she said. "You're me dad, aren't you?"

Dad laughed.

"We're a great team," he said.

He picked Lizzie up and held her above his head. He set off running round the room, holding her up, like she was flying, and Lizzie laughed and laughed, and she yelled, "Are me feet off the floor yet? They are! They are!"

Auntie Doreen stamped her feet.

"Put that girl down!" she yelled.

"But Auntie Doreen," laughed Lizzie, "it's fun!"

Auntie Doreen pulled her hat down. She took a big bite of a dumpling. She stamped towards the door.

"Oh," said Lizzie. "Don't go, Auntie Doreen."

"I am leaving this madhouse, Jackie," said Auntie Doreen. "Elizabeth, this is your very last chance. Come with me now."

Dad lowered Lizzie to the floor.

Lizzie didn't move. She didn't want Auntie Doreen to go off in a huff, but she couldn't leave her dad. She shook her head.

"See what you've done to that girl?" said Auntie Doreen.

Lizzie laughed.

"I'm all right," she said. She smiled at Auntie Doreen, then at Dad. "Mebbe I'll even enter the competition meself. Mebbe I'll make wings for meself."

"We'll enter together!" said Dad. "We'll be a family of human birds!"

"Let's get started," said Lizzie, and they ran out together into the garden. They started gathering feathers from under the trees.

Auntie Doreen stamped out of the door.

"Bye-bye, Auntie Doreen!" shouted Lizzie.

"Bye-bye, Doreen!" shouted Dad.

"I'll bye-bye you!" snapped Auntie Doreen.

She stamped down the garden, through the gate, and slammed it behind her.

"I'll be back!" she said. "And I'll bring somebody that'll clip your wings!"

9

Lizzie and her dad worked all day and
into the night, gathering feathers and string and thread
and bits of cloth and coat-hangers and ribbons and
buttons and beads. They stitched and snipped and stuck.
By the next morning, Lizzie's wings and her beak and her
crest were just about done. Lizzie and Dad stood together
at the door, both of them wearing their wings. They were
worn out, but they were so happy, so proud of themselves.
Lizzie leaned on her dad and said he was right, they
were a fantastic team. Brilliant sunlight slanted over the
rooftops and through the trees and onto their happy and
excited faces. Birds tweeted and whistled all around.
The city traffic rumbled and roared. Dad giggled as he
thought of what they could do next.

"We need a nest, Lizzie," he said.

"A nest?"

"Aye. To make it all proper. To make us like proper
birds."

Lizzie looked into his eyes.

"Go on," he said. "It'll make me happy."

She smiled and shrugged and said, "OK, Dad. What'll
we need?"

Well, they needed grass and twigs and straw and
leaves and string, and ripped-up tea towels, and bits of old

shirt and bits of old jumper, and dusters and holey socks, and feathers, and carpet fluff. They carried all the bits and pieces into the kitchen, and they knelt on the floor and put everything together into the shape of a nest. Lizzie smiled and hummed as they worked. Dad tweeted and whistled and cawed.

"Isn't it lovely?" he said. "A proper little home for us."

He reached into his pocket and found a worm. He held it up and let it dangle from his fingers, then he gobbled it up.

"Would you like one, Lizzie?"

She shook her head.

"I'll have these instead," she said, and she nibbled some peanuts.

Dad stood up on tiptoes and stretched his wings up high and pulled his tummy in.

"Look," he said. "I'm getting skinnier already!"

"You can't be!" she laughed, but when she looked more closely, it seemed as if he really was. She poked him and called him tin ribs.

"I'll soon be light as a feather!" he said.

They went on working, carefully shaping the nest into a ring with a deep hollow at the centre.

"Birds is the best in the world at looking after their

little'ns, you know," said Dad. "They bring them up good and strong. They protect them from all dangers."

They worked on, until at last it was finished. Then they stepped into it and sat there wearing their lovely wings, in their home-made nest in the corner of the kitchen, and they beamed with joy.

Dad giggled and wiggled his bottom.

"Oooh!" he said. "I feel an egg coming on."

He laid an imaginary egg. He reached underneath himself, picked it up and held it in the air between their faces. Lizzie took it from his hands. She said it was so beautiful, the bright blue shell, the dappled brown markings on it. Then she gave it back and he put it into the nest again.

"Now I'll sit on it till it hatches," he said. He closed his eyes and concentrated. "Come on, little chick," he whispered. He jumped up. "It worked!" He picked up the imaginary chick and cupped it in his hands and held it to his face. "Hello, little'n," he said. "Isn't he lovely, Lizzie?" Lizzie gazed down into Dad's hands. She smiled.

"He's just gorgeous," she said, and she reached down and touched and stroked the imaginary chick.

Then Dad opened his hands and raised them.

"He's growing up already," he said. "Off you go. Fly away!" The imaginary bird flew from them. Dad pointed around the room and they pretended to see the brand-new bird flying there. "There he is! See! See! See!"

Lizzie giggled.

"Silly man," she said. "Anyway, it's the mams that lay the eggs, not the dads."

"Aye, you're right," said Dad. But he went on pointing and waving until the imaginary chick flew right away. "Bye-bye," he said. "Bye-bye, lovely little'n."

Then they sat silent in the nest again and the afternoon moved on and they dozed and dreamed their dreams of flying.

"I could sit here for ever," said Dad. "Just me and you." But he suddenly jumped up. "But no time for that!

There's a competition to think about! Let's get them tail feathers and beaks and crests done, Lizzie!"

So they set to work again. Lizzie watched her dad, and after a while she said, "Da-ad."

"Aye? What is it, love?"

"Well," she said. "We have to realize. Even with the tail feathers and the beaks and the crests, it might still not … work."

"Eh?" said Dad.

He blinked and shook his head like he didn't understand her, or like he didn't want to understand her.

"But even if it doesn't work," said Lizzie, "it won't really matter. Even if we end up getting fished out of the river, it won't really matter, will it, Dad?"

Dad blinked again and stared at her. He gobbled a worm. He rustled his wings.

"Tweet, tweet!" he said.

Lizzie shook his arm.

"You understand, don't you?" she said. "It might not work. But whatever happens, we'll have done it together, won't we, Dad? That's what really matters."

Dad jumped up and started running around the room, flapping his wings.

"Caw caw!" he yelled. "Caw caw!"

"Dad!" said Lizzie. "Are you listening to me?"

Then there was a yell from outside.

"FINAL ENTRIES FOR THE HUMAN BIRD COMPETITION!"

Lizzie and Dad stood dead still. It came again.

"ANY MORE ENTRIES FOR THE GREAT HUMAN BIRD COMPETITION?"

Dad opened the door. There was chubby little Mr Poop outside the gate with his megaphone and his clipboard.

"ANY MORE ENTRIES FOR—"

"Aye!" shouted Dad. "In here, Mr Poop!"

10

Mr Poop peered at Dad. He came through the gate towards the door.

"But we've got you already, Mr Crow," he said.

"No, it's not me," said Dad. "It's this young'n here."

And he stepped aside and showed Lizzie standing there.

"Aha!" said Mr Poop. "Isn't she rather young for such a dangerous adventure?"

"I'll look after her," said Dad. "Birds is best in the world at looking after their little'ns."

"Hmmmmm," said Mr Poop.

Dad led him inside. Mr Poop narrowed his eyes and looked at Lizzie and clicked his tongue and shook his head.

"She's strong," said Dad. "She's brave. She's the bravest girl in the whole world. Everybody says so, don't they, Lizzie?"

"Do they now?" said Mr Poop.

Lizzie shrugged. She thought about what Mr Mint had said about her, and the things that Auntie Doreen sometimes said, and the things her dad always said. And she thought of her mam, who'd told her she was brave, the very bravest of the brave.

"Sometimes," she said to Mr Poop.

Mr Poop's eyes softened for a moment. "Good girl," he whispered. Then he lifted his clipboard and licked his pencil. "Name?"

"Elizabeth," said Lizzie.

"Eliz-a-beth," said Mr Poop. "Elizabeth what?"

"Elizabeth Crow!" said Dad.

"Elizabeth *what*?" said Lizzie.

"Crow," said Dad. "Caw caw!"

Mr Poop peered at them both.

"Are you sure?"

"Aye," said Dad quickly. "Isn't it, Lizzie?"

"Ye-es," said Lizzie, and she found herself copying her dad and cawing like a crow. "Caw caw! Caw caw!"

Mr Poop wrote it down.

"Occupation?" he asked.

Lizzie shrugged.

"Just girl, I suppose," she said. "I'm a schoolgirl."

"No," said Dad. "You're more than that! You're a *bird-girl*. I'm a birdman, she's a birdgirl. It's in the family."

Mr Poop wrote it down in his chubby writing. He paused. He looked at them again. He peered at Lizzie's wings.

"Method of propulsion? Wings and faith, I suppose?"

"Aye," said Dad. "That's correct. Wings and faith. And the beak and the crest. Show him, Lizzie."

Lizzie put her beak and crest on.

"You'll not have seen nowt like that, have you?" said Dad. "And we'll have tail feathers, just like a proper bird. They're Lizzie's idea. She's a method of propulsion genius!"

Mr Poop inspected Lizzie and Dad. He peered into the nest. He tapped his cheek. He licked his pencil.

"Hmmm," he murmured. "Hmmmmmmmmmm."

He rubbed his chubby tummy.

"Every day there's more of them," he said. "There's a long jump champion on a ship from Madagascar. There's a pole-vaulter coming from Smolensk. There's a trapeze girl from Malta, a cartwheeler from Cuba, and seven whirling dervishes from Tashkent. There's loopers and whoopers and swoopers and hoopers. There's a fella with a million pink elastic bands. There's gliders and slings and ten-foot crossbows and…"

"And there's them like us with wings!" said Dad.

"There is," said Mr Poop. "Sadly, there is." He held out the clipboard and pencil to Lizzie.

"The river is very wet at this time of year, Miss Crow," he said. "Sign here. And here. And also here."

Lizzie signed and smiled.

He inspected her signature. "Entry accepted!" he said, and he signed the form himself. He tucked the clipboard under his arm.

"Do you have any water wings, Miss Crow?" asked Mr Poop.

"Water wings!" scoffed Dad. "Go on, Mr Poop, off you go."

So Mr Poop went out again.

"See you on Sunday!" he called. "Take-off is at 10a.m.!"

Dad closed the door behind him.

"Birdman and Birdgirl," said Dad. "We'll be the greatest fliers the world has ever seen. Yahoo!" He ran around the room, then he stopped and pondered.

"I'll let you win, Lizzie," he said.

"Eh?"

"I will. I'll let you win. Just at the end I'll slow down and you can overtake me. You can swoop right past me and across the line. Yeahhh! Lizzie Crow, Human Bird! Give that lass a thousand pounds!"

They giggled. Then they stopped. They listened.

"There's somebody in the garden," whispered Lizzie.

They tiptoed to the window. They peeked out into the garden.

"Who is it?" whispered Dad.

They could see nothing unusual, just the trees and the shadows gathering under the branches. But there was a rustling sound, and now there seemed to be something moving through the shadows. What was it? Lizzie peered harder, harder, and then she saw a familiar figure out there.

"Oh, it's just Auntie Doreen again," said Lizzie. Then she gasped. "Aagh! And Mr Mint's with her!"

"Quick!" said Dad. "Into the nest!"

11

Auntie Doreen and Mr Mint

hesitated at the door. They pressed their ears against it. Nothing to be heard. Mr Mint shivered.

"Are you sure this is all right, Mrs Doody?" he said.

"Course it's all right," said Auntie Doreen. "The man's barmy as butter. We've got to get the poor girl out of his clutches."

She slowly turned the door handle, slowly opened the door.

"But sneaking into somebody's house..." said Mr Mint. "A man in my position..."

Auntie Doreen dragged him behind her.

"What do they make head teachers from these days?" she said. "Playdough? In my day they were women and men of steel!"

She took a dumpling from her pinny pocket and held it out to him.

"Here," she said. "This'll put some spirit in you."

Mr Mint stared at the strange object.

"What is it?"

Auntie Doreen looked at him in amazement. How could he not know what a dumpling was?

"It's a dumpling, of course!" she said.

"But I don't like dumplings," said Mr Mint.

"Of course you like dumplings. Everybody likes dumplings. Get it down your neck!"

She dragged him inside. She peered around the room. Mr Mint nibbled at the dumpling.

"It's actually quite nice," he said in surprise. He nibbled again. "It's actually quite lovely, Mrs Doody."

"Eh?" grunted Auntie Doreen.

"The dumpling, Mrs Doody," said Mr Mint. "It is quite … delicious."

Auntie Doreen blushed and looked down.

"D'you really think so, Mr Mint?" she said.

"Yes, Mrs Doody."

"Doreen," said Auntie Doreen. "You can call me Doreen."

Now Mr Mint blushed and looked down.

"Thank you, Doreen," he said. He nibbled the dumpling again. "You don't get dumplings like this these days, you know. Not with such a flavour. Not with such … solidity."

"Well, thank you, Mr Mint," said Auntie Doreen.

"Mortimer," he whispered. "Mortimer Mint."

"Mortimer Mint?" echoed Auntie Doreen. "*Mortimer Mint?* You sound like some kind of boiled sweet!"

"That's what my mother used to say. She used to call me Sweetie. Or Polo."

"*Polo?*"

Mr Mint bit his lip.

"You won't tell the children, will you, Doreen? I couldn't stand it if you told the children and they called me Polo at school and—"

Auntie Doreen raised a finger. She narrowed her eyes and peered around the room.

"Hush!" she hissed. "Listen! There's a kind of flipping flapping sound. A kind of rustling sound. There's a kind of whistling tweetling sound."

She gazed around the room. They listened. They heard the lovely birdsong from outside, the distant traffic, the distant rumble and roar of the city. They heard their own breathing. They heard their own beating thumping hearts. They stood in silence, half-entranced. Mr Mint smiled. He whistled softly with the birds. He raised his arms, as if he were about to fly.

"It's just the birds, Doreen," he said.

Auntie Doreen clicked her tongue.

"Just the birds? That's just the blithering point, Mr Mortimer Mint. There's odd things going on in this house. Strange things, peculiar things. Shenanigans with feathers and beaks and wings. And I'm not having it!" Something buzzed past her nose. She jumped. "Oh, pump! What was that?"

"A little fly, that's all," said Mr Mint. He tapped Auntie Doreen on the arm. "You won't tell, will you?"

Auntie Doreen blinked.

"Tell what? Tell who?"

"The children. About *Polo*," he whispered.

"Don't be such a wazzock, Mortimer. Now, what we've got to do is find that poor lass. Look at the mess she lives in. Look at that heap of rubbish on the floor!"

She tiptoed around the room, crept closer to the pile of rubbish. It was the nest, of course. Auntie Doreen's eyes widened. She pointed at it. Lizzie and Dad sat there dead still, their wings folded over their heads.

"Didn't I say there was shenanigans?" she hissed.

She tiptoed closer. She leaned down. Mr Mint followed her. He leaned down.

Then Dad suddenly jumped up and flapped his wings and croaked, "Caw caw! Caw caw! Caw caw!"

And Mr Mint squealed and leapt towards the door.

12

Auntie Doreen caught him by his collar and hauled him back. Dad flapped and cawed in front of them.

"This is the culprit!" said Auntie Doreen. "This is the one that's leading your pupil astray! This is the birdman!"

Mr Mint put out his hand and said, "Very nice to meet you again, Mr—"

"Caw! Caw!" said Dad. "Caw! Caw!"

He poked his beak at Mr Mint. Mr Mint set off for the door again.

"Mortimer!" Auntie Doreen yelled. "POLO!"

Mr Mint stopped. He looked down at the ground.

"Go on, then," said Auntie Doreen. "Give Lizzie's father a piece of your mind."

Mr Mint said nothing. He rubbed his eyes.

"Do it, man," said Auntie Doreen. "Tell him why you're here. Blitheration! You're a head teacher, man!"

Lizzie unfolded her wings and stepped out from the nest. She came slowly towards them.

"Elizabeth," said Auntie Doreen, "come here. We've come to take you away from all this. Mortimer, take charge of your pupil."

Lizzie flapped her wings.

"Caw caw!" she called.

"Look at her," said Auntie Doreen. "Listen to her. Elizabeth! What's seven add two add six add eight add five? *See?* It's all slipping. Spell Czechoslovakia. *See?* No answer. The girl's on her way to rack and ruin."

"Caw caw!" said Lizzie. "Caw caw caw caw caw caw!"

She pretended to run at Mr Mint, then she paused and smiled at him. She was sure he'd understand.

She spoke softly. "I'm only staying off school to look after me dad, Mr Mint."

"Look after him?" squeaked Auntie Doreen. "The man wants locking up!"

"Take no notice of Auntie Doreen," said Lizzie. "She's a bit daft sometimes."

"She's what?" squawked Auntie Doreen.

Lizzie flapped towards Auntie Doreen and kissed her on the cheek.

"But she's lovely, really." She smiled as Auntie Doreen gasped, then she turned to Mr Mint again. "I'll be back at school next Monday, after the competition."

Dad pulled his beak off.

"Well said, Lizzie," he said. "Go on then, Doreen. Go on, Mr Mint. Off you go!"

Mr Mint smiled and turned to leave. Auntie Doreen watched him in amazement.

"Is that it?" she thundered. "Have you really got nothing else to say to them? You're a man of distinction. A man with authority. A man who can take control!"

Mr Mint sighed. He pondered. He tapped his head and stroked his chin. He turned back again. He carefully inspected Dad's wings and Lizzie's wings. He sighed again and pondered again. Everyone waited.

"Do you think it'll work?" he asked.

"*What?*" squawked Auntie Doreen.

"Course it will," said Dad. "These is wonderful wings we've made, Mr Mint."

Mr Mint went on pondering.

"I suppose," he murmured, "if you run fast enough and jump high enough, and flap hard enough…"

He trotted a circle around the room. He made little jumps and tried flapping his arms.

"That's the idea," said Dad. "D'you want to try me wings on?"

"Mortimer!" squeaked Auntie Doreen. She hurled a dumpling at him. It flew past him and thudded into the wall and stuck there.

"We're going to have tail feathers as well," said Dad. "They're Lizzie's idea."

"Aha!" said Mr Mint. "A very good idea, Elizabeth. She's such a clever girl, you know." He pondered deeply. "It's the bones, isn't it? Birds' bones are lighter than ours. So in order to compensate we have to—"

"MORTIMER!" snapped Auntie Doreen. "POLO!"

Mr Mint took no notice.

"Of course," he went on, "there are examples of creatures of weight which are able to glide or fly…" He unstuck the dumpling from the

wall. He threw it up and down to test the weight of it. "Interesting problems, Mr … Crow. I suspect you're learning a great deal, Elizabeth."

He pondered the dumpling. "If one could find a way of being thrown with sufficient force…" He leaned back, drew back his arm, and hurled the dumpling across the room. It whizzed past Auntie Doreen's head and thudded once more onto the wall. Mr Mint smiled. "Is it still possible to enter this competition?"

"Course it is," said Dad. "The fella was just here this morning. Get your name down now, Mr Mint."

Mr Mint nodded and pondered. Auntie Doreen grabbed his arm and drew him towards the door.

"Goodbye, Auntie Doreen!" called Lizzie. "Lovely to see you. Goodbye, Mr Mint. See you on Monday."

"Or even Sunday!" said Mr Mint.

"That'd be great!" said Lizzie.

"The flying head teacher!" said Dad.

Auntie Doreen sighed.

"The world's gone mad," she groaned.

Lizzie suddenly remembered what Auntie Doreen had asked her.

"Oh, and Auntie Doreen?"

"What?"

"It's twenty-eight!" said Lizzie.

Auntie Doreen goggled at her.

"Seven add two add six add eight add five," said Lizzie. "The answer's twenty-eight. And Czechoslovakia. That's C-Z-E-C-H—"

"Correct!" called Mr Mint. "Good girl, Elizabeth!"

But Auntie Doreen just clamped her hands across her ears.

"It has," she said. "The world's gone mad!"

13

Dad and Lizzie watched Auntie Doreen and Mr Mint leave the garden. Then they closed the door.

"Poor Auntie Doreen," said Lizzie.

"Aye," said Dad. "Poor Auntie Doreen. Mr Mint's a lovely bloke, isn't he?"

"He is," said Lizzie. She giggled and held her hand over her mouth. "Polo Mint!" she whispered.

"Polo Mint!" said Dad.

The day was darkening. They looked through the window towards the sunset, glowing through the trees and over the rooftops of the city.

"Time's flying," said Dad. He smiled. He pointed into the air. "There it is, flying past! Catch it!" And he jumped, and caught Time in his hands, and showed it to Lizzie. She took it from him, and threw it up again.

"There it goes," she called. "Bye-bye. Bye-bye, Time!"

They gazed out. The sky began to burn bright red and yellow and orange and it was so beautiful.

Dad sang.

> *"Evening's coming on,*
> *Like a lovely buttered scone.*
> *Night will soon appear,*
> *Like a little fish's ear.*

Then all will be dark
Like in the tummy of the shark.
And then we will sleep
With the farmer's sheep.
And we will be happy
Like a soft new-washed nappy."

Lizzie clapped softly.

"That's lovely, Dad," she whispered.

She joined in and they sang the song again.

"I made it up meself," said Dad.

"You're such a clever dad, Dad."

Soon the sun was all gone and the darkness crept right across the inky sky and the stars began to shine. An owl hooted, then another.

"I love the night," said Lizzie.

"Me too," said Dad. "And you're right, you know."

"What about?"

"You're right," he said again. "It doesn't matter if we fly or if we fall. We've got each other. We're doing it together. That's all that matters."

Lizzie smiled.

"Yes," she whispered. "That's all that matters."

Silver moonlight shone into the room. The owls

hooted, and somewhere a night bird sang. Lizzie and Dad sang again and they danced to their own song, and to the song of the birds. They moved softly across the floor. They raised their arms and beat their wings and they sang and whistled and cooed, and at times they had to look downwards to make sure that their feet weren't really off the floor.

And then they slept, and dreamed the dreams of birds.

14

"ROLL UP! ROLL UP!

IT'S TIME FOR THE GREAT HUMAN BIRD COMPETITION!"

Mr Poop's voice echoed through the streets, off the walls and off the rooftops. It echoed through the city.

"ROLL UP! ROLL UP!"

Dad and Lizzie were fast asleep. Mr Poop's voice rang and echoed through their dreams.

"ROLL UP! ROLL UP!"

"What's that?" said Dad.

"What day is it?" said Lizzie.

"IT'S THE DAY OF THE GREAT HUMAN BIRD COMPETITION!"

called Mr Poop.

"Oh no!" said Dad.

"We're not ready!" said Lizzie.

She tottered to the window. There was chubby little Mr Poop with his megaphone in the street outside.

"They've come from Bikini Atoll and Baton Rouge! They've come from Chattanooga and Châteauneuf! Look! There's the Dragonfly Woman from Dubai! And the Human Helicopter, Hubert Hall!"

"Dad! We're going to be late!" said Lizzie.

They struggled to adjust their wings. They put on their beaks and crests and their tailpieces.

"There's Benny the Bee Boy all the way from Burramurra!" yelled Mr Poop. "Come along! The competition is about to begin! Roll up! ROLL UP!"

"We're ready!" yelled Dad. "Lizzie, get your wings on proper! Are mine looking right?"

He opened the door and yelled again.

"We're nearly ready, Mr Poop!"

"Then come along, COME ALONG!" said Mr Poop.

"Is it true?" shouted Lizzie. "That there's all those people from all those places?"

Mr Poop looked astonished.

"Of course it is!" he answered.  "Do you think you're dreaming it? Look, there goes Elastic Eddie from Elsmere Port! And Danny the Dart from Donegal! Whirligig Winnie from Wye! Come and see Bouncing Bess from Baffin Bay! Soaring Sid from… Come along! Hurry up! Come and join in!"

"Ready, Dad?" said Lizzie.

"Ready, Lizzie," said Dad.

"How do I look?" said Lizzie.

"Perfect," said Dad. "Me?"

"Like a birdman," said Lizzie.

They hugged each other.

"Just think," said Dad. "If only your mam could see us now."

They flapped their wings. They waved into the sky.

"Hello, Mam!" they called softly. "Hello, love!"

Then they took a deep breath, hugged each other, and they ran out through the door.

15

"DON'T DO IT!"

It was Auntie Doreen, trotting in through the gate.

"Oh, Doreen," said Dad. "Don't be such a fussypants!"

"Don't do it, Lizzie," said Auntie Doreen. "He's daft as a doughnut!"

"No he's not," said Lizzie. "He's lovely." She kissed Auntie Doreen's cheek. "And so are you."

"Jackie, man! Lizzie! How do you spell pneumatisation? What's twenty add eight add seven add three add six? *See?* No answers! Your brain's all blithered! Don't do it, lass!"

Lizzie and Dad laughed and ran past her towards Mr Poop.

"Here they are!" yelled Mr Poop. "Make way for the Crows! Here they are, Leaping Lizzie and Jumping Jack, the flying folk from down your way! The Human Bird Competition! TIME FOR THE GREAT HUMAN BIRD COMPETITION!"

"Oh, the wazzocks," said Auntie Doreen "The blithering boops. The nits, the ninnies, the nincompoopy noodleheads!"

She gasped as Mr Mint rushed past the gate with fireworks tied to his bottom and a pointy helmet on his head. He blew her a kiss as he passed by.

"And the soaring head teacher, Missile Mint!" yelled Mr Poop. "Let him through! Make way! Make way!"

Mr Poop saw Auntie Doreen standing there. He came to the garden gate.

"Any last minute entries?" he called. He widened his eyes. "What about you, madam?"

"Me?" croaked Auntie Doreen.

"Yes, madam, you! Come and join us. Tell us your name, your method of propulsion! Don't hold back. Step with others into the sky!"

Auntie Doreen dug into her pinny. She hurled a dumpling at Mr Poop, who ducked and giggled.

"Aha!" he yelled. "Is it Dumpling Dora from Dungeness?"

She hurled another dumpling at him, then rushed into the house. She got her suet, her flour, her eggs, her water. She put them in a bowl and started stirring and mixing and bashing and singing.

"Dumplings, dumplings, lovely lovely dumplings…"

Outside, the competition started.

"OUR FIRST COMPETITOR!" yelled Mr Poop. "Woodpecker Wallie, all the way from Whitley Bay!"

Auntie Doreen stopped and listened.

"It's mad," she said. "It's impossible. Nobody could possibly—"

"FIVE!" called Mr Poop. "FOUR ... THREE ... TWO ... ONE! There he goes, folks!"

A drum rolled. The crowd roared. Auntie Doreen shut her eyes and prayed.

"Go on, Wallie!" yelled Mr Poop. "Oh YES...! OH YES...! Oh no!"

There was a great big splash.

"Never mind, Wallie!" yelled Mr Poop. "Who's next in line?"

16

Auntie Doreen mixed and stirred and whacked and bashed.

"Dumplings!" she sang. "Lovely lovely dumplings…"

She kept pausing, shaking.

"Me brain's bending and buckling," she said. "Me mind's twisting and twockling. Me heart's thundering and thumpling. Oh, hecky hicky heck…"

But her eyes were drawn to the window, to the competition. Her ears were tugged by Mr Poop's voice.

"What a wonderful machine," called Mr Poop. "What a creation, what an invention, what a device!"

Auntie Doreen could see nothing. She stood on tiptoes, but saw nothing, just the trees and the empty sky.

"Are you ready?" called Mr Poop.

Auntie Doreen couldn't stop herself. She ran outside. She climbed up into a cherry tree.

"Pedal hard, madam!" yelled Mr Poop. "Pedal fast!"

Auntie Doreen struggled higher. She stared towards the sky above the river.

"Pedal harder!" yelled Mr Poop. "Pedal faster! *Faster! Faster!* She's away!"

And yes! There it was, a bicycle with wings plunging through the sky. And a woman on it, pedalling so fast her

feet couldn't be seen. And a crowd was yelling, cheering, whooping.

"Faster!" yelled Mr Poop. "Faster than that, madam! That's the style! OH YES...!"

But the bicycle staggered, stuttered and dropped, and there was a mighty crash and a mighty splash and a roar of disappointment from the crowd.

"OH NO!" yelled Mr Poop. "Ah well! Fish her out, lads! Better luck next time, madam. And now look! It's Elastic Eddie! Here he comes!"

There was a gasp of excitement, a murmur, a hush, the roll of a drum.

Auntie Doreen scrambled higher. At last she could see through to the river. She saw the crowds on either bank. And she saw Elastic Eddie in his blue rubber suit and his yellow helmet. She saw him wave to the crowd, then rest his back against an enormous catapult made of a million pink elastic bands. She saw the assistants pulling back the catapult, stretching it tighter, tighter.

"That's right, lads," called Mr Poop. "Get those elastic bands tight. Pull harder. Are you comfortable, Eddie? Are you ready, Eddie?"

Eddie did a thumbs-up. He stepped backwards, backwards as the catapult stretched behind him.

"Excellent!" called Mr Poop. "Stand clear, ladies and gentlemen. OK, lads. Five, four, three… No not yet! Not yet!" But the lads couldn't take the strain, they let go too early. "Hold on, Eddie!" yelled Mr Poop. But Eddie was off, and out of control, and cartwheeling through the empty air.

"Uurgh!" groaned Auntie Doreen.

"AARGH!" groaned Mr Poop. "OH NO!"

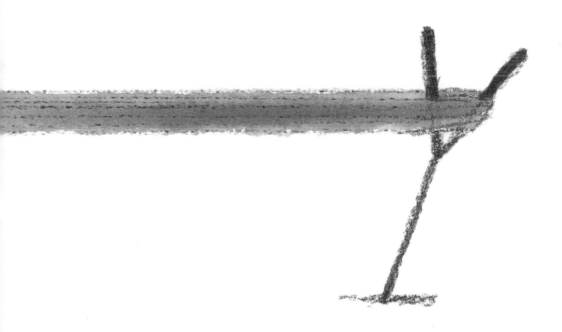

And there was a groan, a crash, an enormous splash, and Mr Poop calling, "Bad luck Eddie! Ah well, fish him out! And now, Lenny the Lop, the Human Flea!"

Auntie Doreen looked down. She trembled. She'd climbed so high. How would she ever get down again?

"If anybody can do it, Lenny can!" yelled Mr Poop.

"Don't do it!" yelled Auntie Doreen. "It's crackers! It's crazy! It can't be done! Get me down!"

"Off you go, lad! Leap, Lenny, leap! Good lad! Higher! Higher! Leap for the... Oh crikey!"

Scream and groan and splash and crash and "Fish him out lads. Hard luck, Lenny! Who's the next in line?" and Auntie Doreen all alone in the cherry tree yelling, "Help! Help! Get me down!"

17

Out on the riverbank, Lizzie and Dad waited. They trembled with excitement. They roared encouragement and gasped with disappointment. They kept jumping up and practising little leaps and runs. They flapped their wings. They waved at the crowd.

Benny the Bee Boy buzzed over their heads and down into the river. Winnie whirled her whirligig and whizzed into the water. Bouncing Bess came bouncing inside a huge ball down a long steep ramp and straight into the drink. Soaring Sid soared from a steeple, turned three somersaults and did a perfect swallow dive into the Tyne. The Human Helicopter Hubert Hall stepped from a rooftop, hung in the air while the home-made helicopter blades whizzed around his head for two seconds, then dropped like a stone. And all the time the crowd yelled and dogs barked and cats howled and seagulls screamed and Mr Poop stood at the top of a tall stepladder and held the megaphone to his mouth and kept up an endless stream of advice.

"Higher!
    Harder!
        Faster!
            Braver!
Yes! Yes! At last! Yahoo!
Oh dear! Oh no! Oh heck!
Fish him out! Fish her out!
Who's next?
Wonderful!
    Marvellous!
        Just amazing!
That's the style!
Oh cripes! Oh yes! Oh no!
What a creation!
Oh crikey!
    Oh blinking no!"

And crashes and splashes and
yells and sighs, until at last
the call.

"THE CROWS!" yelled Mr Poop. "It's time for the Crows! Make way for the feathery father and his leaping lass!"

Lizzie and Dad sprang to their feet. The crowd roared.

"Look at the work that's gone into those wings!" called Mr Poop. "What invention! What imagination! Will they do it? Roar them onwards, ladies and gentlemen! Roar them upwards!"

But Lizzie hesitated.

"What about Auntie Doreen?" she said.

"What *about* Auntie Doreen?" said Dad.

"We can't do this and not let Auntie Doreen see," said Lizzie.

They both looked back towards home.

"Auntie Doreen!" shouted Lizzie. "AUNTIE DOREEN! IT'S OUR TURN!"

But Auntie Doreen knew it was their turn, and she was trembling in the tree with her eyes squeezed tight shut and her hands clamped across her ears.

"Come along!" called Mr Poop. "Fortune favours the brave!"

"Come on!" yelled the crowd.

"Come on!" yelled the other competitors.

"Come on," said Lizzie to her dad, and she set off running homewards.

"Give us a couple of minutes!" yelled Dad to Mr Poop.

They sprinted to the gate, into the garden, through the door, into the kitchen. Nobody there! They gasped. They searched. They yelled for her. Where was Auntie Doreen? Then they heard a funny squawking from outside, and they looked. Auntie Doreen was in the cherry tree! They ran out and stood beneath her. Dad looked up in astonishment.

"Doreen," he said. "What on earth are you doing in the cherry tree?"

"Never mind that now," said Lizzie. "It's our turn, Auntie Doreen! You have to come and see us fly!"

Mr Poop's voice echoed across the rooftops.

"THE CROWS! WHAT'S HAPPENED TO THE CROWS? THEY MUST COME BACK OR THEY'LL BE DISQUALIFIED!"

"Please, Auntie Doreen! Please!" said Lizzie.

"But it's all—" said Auntie Doreen.

"Never mind what it is," said Lizzie. "If we don't get back now and you don't come with us it'll all come to nowt!"

"LIZZIE! JACKIE!" yelled Mr Poop. "WHERE ON EARTH ARE THE CROWS?"

"Please!" said Dad.

"Please!" said Lizzie.

"HAVE THEY LOST THEIR NERVE?" yelled Mr Poop.

Auntie Doreen looked down at them.

"But I can't get down," she said in a little voice.

"LIZZIE! JACKIE! COME BACK NOW!"

"Jump," said Lizzie. "Jump, Auntie Doreen, jump!"

"BE BRAVE!" yelled Mr Poop.

And Auntie Doreen took a deep breath, said a quick prayer, and jumped, and dropped like a dumpling to their side.

18

Back they trotted and sprinted to the river. The crowd roared with relief and delight.

"WELL DONE!" called Mr Poop. "I KNEW YOU WOULDN'T LET US DOWN. STAND ASIDE! MAKE WAY FOR THE CROWS!"

Lizzie and Dad held hands, ready to begin.

"Wish us well, Auntie Doreen," said Lizzie.

"Tell us you hope we'll be OK," said Dad.

"JACKIE!" yelled Mr Poop. "LIZZIE!"

"Give us a hug," said Lizzie.

"Give us a kiss," said Dad.

"Tell us you love us and you hope we'll be OK."

"COME ALONG!" called Mr Poop.

Dad and Lizzie gazed at Auntie Doreen. Auntie Doreen gazed at them.

"Aye," she whispered. "I love you both. And I hope you'll be OK."

"We're ready, Mr Poop!" yelled Dad.

"AT LAST, THE CROWS ARE READY! GET THE RAMP UP, LADS!"

The assistants raised a ramp at the river's edge. A drummer started drumming. The crowd murmured with excitement.

"Give them plenty space now," said Mr Poop, more softly. "Stand aside! *Wings and faith!*" he whispered through his megaphone. "Nothing fancy for the crows. No machines or engines or slings or elastic bands. Wings and faith and hope and … dare I say it? … love!"

The ramp was ready. It slanted upwards. Its end hung over the water. Dad and Lizzie stepped onto it, poised to run. Auntie Doreen peeked out between her fingers. Her heart was thundering and thumping. Her brain was tweakling and twockling.

"Look at the look in their eyes," murmured Mr Poop.
"Look at those courageous smiles. Hard work, concentra-
tion, wings and faith! And love, ladies and gentlemen.
Love! If anybody deserves this prize, the Crows do."

"Please," whispered Auntie Doreen. She clenched her
fists and squeezed her eyes. "Please, Jackie. Please, Lizzie.
Do it. Fly!"

"Are you ready?" called Mr Poop. "Are you steady?"

Dad gave a thumbs-up. Lizzie gave a thumbs-up.
They grinned at each other.

"Ten…" said Mr Poop.

"Nine …

eight …

seven …

six …

five… We're with you all the way, Jackie! Bon voyage, Lizzie!"

The crowd rumbled and roared. The drum rolled.

"GO ON!" they yelled. "DO IT, JACKIE! DO IT, LIZZIE!"

"The sky's the limit!" called Mr Poop. "FOUR …

THREE …

TWO …

ONE …

THEY'RE OFF!"

And Lizzie and her dad started running towards the river, so fast, so hard, so filled with courage and hope. They flapped their wings as they approached the end of the ramp. They reached for the sky. They leapt. And it was so weird, so wild, so wonderful. Lizzie looked at her dad leaping at her side. She looked into the wide blue sky and the city stretching out all around them. They flapped their wings and they roared with laughter at the joy and the craziness of it.

Auntie Doreen couldn't watch. She shut her eyes.

"GO ON!" yelled Mr Poop.

"AYE, GO ON!" yelled the crowd.

"YES!

YES!

YES!"

"AAAARGH!"

yelled Mr Poop, as Dad faltered, as he dropped. But Lizzie just laughed even more and flapped harder, harder, harder.

"It doesn't matter, Dad!" she called.

"Do it on your own, Lizzie!" he yelled back at her. "Keep going. Fly!"

But then Lizzie herself began to fall.

"AAARGH!" yelled Mr Poop. "OH NO!"

"OH NO!" yelled the crowd.

And she fell into the river with a mighty splash.

"OH DEAR!" yelled Mr Poop. "Ah, well. Better luck next time, Crows. Fish them out! Who's the next in line?"

On the riverbank, Auntie Doreen stamped her feet.

"Pittle paddle pump," she said. "Oh, puddly pittlepot. Pump pump pump and pittle pump."

She stayed for a moment. She watched Lizzie and Dad swim back to land, then she trotted back to the kitchen and her dumplings.

19

Auntie Doreen made a whole tray of
smooth white shiny steaming dumplings. They were the
best she'd ever made, white as snow, heavy as lead. They
lay there on the kitchen table, waiting for Lizzie and Dad
to come home.

"These'll calm them down," she said to herself.
"These'll bring them down to earth." She wiped a tear
from her eye. She stretched her arms towards the sky, then
let them slowly fall. "Oh, the poor souls," she whispered to
herself.

Not long after, she heard the garden gate open. She
heard footsteps in the garden. Lizzie and Dad came
through the door, all soaked, all sodden, with the
drenched wings hanging heavily at their sides.

"Hello, Auntie Doreen," said Lizzie.

"Hello, Doreen," said Dad. "We're back."

"Come on," said Auntie Doreen. "In you come. Get
them wet wings off."

She helped to take them off and hung them carefully
on the back of the kitchen door.

"Look," she said. "I've got some nice fresh dumplings
for you here."

"Lovely," said Dad.

"Lovely," said Lizzie.

She put towels around their shoulders. They all sat at the table and nibbled the dumplings. Outside, the day began to darken, and Dad and Lizzie quietly began their song.

"Evening's coming on,
Like a lovely buttered scone.
Night will soon appear,
Like a little fish's ear.
Then all will be dark
Like in the tummy of the shark.
And we will all sleep
With the farmer's sheep.
And we will be happy
Like a soft new-washed nappy."

"That's a pretty song," said Auntie Doreen.

"Thank you," said Dad. "I made it up meself."

"Such a clever man," said Auntie Doreen.

Then Lizzie whispered dreamily, "Forty-four."

"What's forty-four?" said Auntie Doreen.

"The sum you gave me: twenty add eight add seven add three add six," said Lizzie. "It's forty-four. And pneumatisation is P-N-E-U-M—"

"Correct," said Auntie Doreen. "Well, I think it is. You're such a clever lass."

They continued to eat and sing, then Dad leaned back in his chair.

"These is…" he said. "Ahem. Doreen, these is in fact very nice dumplings."

"Oh, Jackie," said Auntie Doreen. "You're a lovely lad, really. Here, have another."

Lizzie and Dad grew warmer and happier. They sighed and smiled, and at last Lizzie couldn't hold it in.

"Oh!" she gasped. "It was so *brilliant*! It was so… Oh!"

"It was *wonderful*!" said Dad. "It was *great*! It was so…"

"Oh we ran so *fast*!" said Lizzie.

"And we jumped so *high*!"

"And we flapped so *hard*!"

"And we reached for the *sky*!"

"And the air was so *clear*!"

"And so *cool*!"

They looked with joy at each other. They looked with joy into their memories and their dreams.

"And it didn't *matter*!" said Dad. "It didn't matter when I fell!"

"I just *laughed*!" said Lizzie. "It didn't matter when *I* fell!"

"I laughed an' all," said Dad. "Oh, and the *water*…"

"So *wet*!" laughed Lizzie.

"So *cold*!"

"So…"

They jumped from their chairs. They started doing a bird dance around the table.

"Come on, Doreen!" said Dad.

"Join in, Auntie Doreen!" said Lizzie.

And the door opened, and Mr Mint was standing there, drenched as well, with the bum of his trousers all burned out.

20

"**Mortimer!**" said Auntie Doreen. "You an' all?"

"Yes, me an' all, Doreen."

He splashed towards them, shaking his head.

"But oh!" he said. "It was so *wonderful*! It was so *brilliant*! Flap flap splash! Flap flap splash!"

He giggled.

"Have a dumpling," said Auntie Doreen.

"Lovely," he said. "Delicious, Doreen!"

"We're dancing," said Lizzie. "Come on, join in!"

And Mr Mint ate his dumpling and joined in with the dance around the table.

"Come on, Doreen," he said, and he reached out for her hand.

"But the dumplings is getting cold," she said.

Mr Mint drew her closer.

"You'll love it once you start," he said.

And at last Auntie Doreen moved from the table and joined in.

"That's right, Auntie Doreen!" said Lizzie.

"That's the way to do it!" said Dad.

She danced faster and harder and she giggled and laughed.

"You look great," said Mr Mint. "You look *lovely*!"

"Are me feet off the floor?" yelled Auntie Doreen. "Are me feet off the floor yet?"

"They are!" yelled Lizzie. "They are, Auntie Doreen! **They really are!**"

David Almond is known worldwide as the Carnegie, Whitbread and Smarties award-winning author of *Skellig*, *The Fire-Eaters* and many other novels, stories and plays. *My Dad's A Birdman* is his first novel for younger readers, which he describes as "a fast and lively book filled with humour and hope … a true children's book".

David grew up in a big, busy family in a coal-mining town on the river Tyne, where stories were part of life. "I always knew I'd be a writer – I wrote stories and stitched them into little books. I had aunts and uncles who could have a room of folk in fits of laughter and tears with their tales. I loved our local library and dreamed of seeing books with my name on the cover. I also dreamed of playing for Newcastle United (and I still wait for the call)."

David lives in Northumberland with his family, and writes in a cabin at the bottom of his garden, where he makes tea and is visited by the birds.

"He has the exquisite ability to describe the nature of love and the constant wonder of being alive."

The Whitbread Judges

Polly Dunbar studied illustration at Brighton Art School. She is the author/illustrator of *Dog Blue*, *Flyaway Katie*, *Here's A Little Poem* and *Penguin*. She says, "*My Dad's A Birdman* was great to illustrate. It's so funny and colourful, as well as being poignant."

Polly lives and works in Brighton. She thinks that colour is a brilliant way to cheer yourself up and whenever she's feeling grey, she puts on her best pink frock and paints! When she's not illustrating, she likes to make puppets.

About *Flyaway Katie:*
"Magical and beautiful." *The Guardian*